when
DINOS

AURS

came with everything

written by Elise Broach
illustrated by David Small

Atheneum Books for Young Readers • New York   London   Toronto   Sydney

Atheneum Books for Young Readers • An imprint of Simon
& Schuster Children's Publishing Division • 1230 Avenue of
the Americas, New York, New York 10020 • Text copyright
© 2007 by Elise Broach • Illustrations copyright © 2007
by David Small • All rights reserved, including the right of
reproduction in whole or in part in any form. • Book design
by Dan Potash • The text for this book is set in P22 Stanyan
Bold. • The illustrations for this book are rendered in
watercolor and ink. • Manufactured in China •
6 8 10 9 7
Library of Congress Cataloging-in-Publication Data •
Broach, Elise. • When dinosaurs came with everything/
Elise Broach ; illustrated by David Small.—1st ed. • p.
cm. • Summary: Although his mother is a little worried,
a young boy is delighted to discover that every shop in
town is giving away real dinosaurs to their customers. •
ISBN-13: 978-0-689-86922-8 • ISBN-10: 0-689-86922-3
• [1. Dinosaurs—Fiction. 2. Mothers and sons—Fiction.
3. Humorous stories.] • I. Small, David, 1945– ill. II. Title.
• PZ7.B78083Whe 2006 • [E]—dc22 2005011612

For Ward, in honor of
all our family trips
to the American Museum
of Natural History
—E. B.

To Lily
—D. S.

Friday is errand day.

My mom goes on boring errands, and I have to go with her.

And this Friday seemed like every other
Friday . . . until we got to the bakery. A sign
above the doughnuts read:

I couldn't believe my eyes. Neither could my mom.
"They must mean a toy," she said.

But when I took the box of doughnuts, the lady
behind the counter said, "Hold on, little guy.
Don't forget your dinosaur."

And
there
he was!

"Mom!" I yelled. It was a triceratops.

"What!" cried my mom. She did not look happy.
"How are we supposed to get *that* home?"
    The bakery lady smiled. "Oh, don't worry, he'll follow you. They always do."

And he did . . . all the way to the doctor's office, where I had to go for my checkup.

My mom shook her head. "What are we going to do with him now?" She looked him up and down.

That took a while.

"We can't bring him inside," she said finally. "He'll have to stay in the parking lot."

I told him not to talk to strangers.

After my checkup, I asked for a sticker, like usual.
"No stickers today," said the nurse. "Just dinosaurs.
With a shot, you get two."

"I want a shot," I said.

The nurse smiled. "Not today, buddy. But you can
pick up your dinosaur at the front desk."

"Mom!" I yelled. There, at the front desk,
was a stegosaurus.
  "What on earth is going on?" my mom cried.
  "It's a special day," the nurse explained.
"Today, dinosaurs come with everything!"

  "Yessss!" I said.
  "Noooo," my mom groaned.

We walked down the street, and my triceratops and my
stegosaurus walked right behind us.

THUD, THUD, THUD.

They made friends right away.

Across the street, other kids had dinosaurs too. I saw an ankylosaur, a duckbill, and a velociraptor. We all waved at each other. Our mothers glared and kept on walking.

"I think we'd better go home right now," my mom said.
"But what about my haircut? The barber's waiting for me."

My mom looked at the dinosaurs. Then she looked at my bangs.
"The barber always gives you a balloon, doesn't he? A nice balloon?"
"Uh-huh," I said.
I didn't want a balloon.
I wanted a barosaur.

At the barbershop, I gave my triceratops and my stegosaurus doughnuts for a snack. They waited outside and watched through the glass.

The barber pumped the chair up high. He cut my hair too short, but I didn't mind, because then he patted my head and said, "Wait right here, sport."

He was gone for a long time. My mom tapped her foot. "I don't like this," she said. "Where exactly do they keep the balloons?"

Just then, the barber came back with something flying over his head. It wasn't a balloon.

"Mom!" I yelled. It was a pterosaur.

"This is too much," my mom protested.

"Now, listen," she said to the barber. "I think a balloon will
do just fine today. Don't you have any balloons?"
"Sorry, lady. No balloons. You get one of these instead."

It was like that everywhere we went.
At the shoe store, the sign read: BUY TWO PAIR, GET DINOSAUR FREE!
My mom decided my shoes would last a while longer.

At the theater, we could hear the popcorn man shouting,
"Butter? No butter? You want a dinosaur with that?"
My mom said we'd go to the movies another day.

At the diner, I wanted to stop for a hamburger.

But then a girl walked out
with a *Tyrannosaurus rex.*

"Okay, that's it!" my mom cried. "We are definitely not having lunch there."

She looked at my triceratops, my stegosaurus, and my pterosaur. "What are we supposed to do with all of these dinosaurs? We don't have room for them! We can't take care of them!"

I hugged her leg. "Don't worry, Mom. They can live in the backyard!"

My mom shook her head. "Sweetheart, they're not toys.
Dinosaurs are a lot of work."

"But, Mom, look! They eat anything. And they sleep outside.
I'll do everything, I promise. Please, Mom? Please?"

My mom sighed.

"Well, I suppose we can't just leave them here. Thank
heavens we didn't stop at the diner."

We hurried home, and my dinosaurs hurried after us.

THUD, THUD, THUD. FLAP, FLAP, FLAP.

When we were almost there, we saw a little duckbill dinosaur, standing alone on the street corner. He looked lost.

"Mom, that's a baby hadrosaur. He's all by himself!"

"Sweetie, we've already got our hands full."

The hadrosaur followed us.
It wasn't my fault.

When we got home, my mom needed to lie down,
so I made lunch for the dinosaurs.

Then I showed them where to go to the bathroom.

I told them to stay out of the neighbor's
yard because of his mean dog.

And I showed them my slide, my tire swing,
and all the toys in the garage.

They seemed to be having fun, but they really went
wild when I took out my Frisbee.

The hadrosaur had the first throw. The Frisbee landed
on the roof. I saw my mom watching from the window.

"Is everything all right out there?" she asked.

"Everything's fine, Mom. We can get it down." And my
pterosaur flew up and plucked the Frisbee out of the gutter.

My mom kept watching.
She looked at him for a long time.

The next thing I knew, she had him cleaning the gutters!

Then she came out to the backyard with a pile of wet clothes.
"These spikes come in handy, don't they," she said.

Pretty soon, my mom had thought
of chores for all of my dinosaurs.

But I knew they didn't mind. It just
meant they were part of the family.

When we were finished helping, my mom said I could invite some friends over. It was a bring-your-own-dinosaur party!

And guess what happened next?

I heard my mom on the phone to the bakery.
She asked, "Do you have any doughnuts left?"

And that's when I knew
everything would be just fine.